HOUGHTON MIFFLIN

The Literature Experience

READING

Celebrate Reading with us!

Cover and title page illustrations from *The Little Bear Book* by Anthony Browne.
Copyright © 1988 by Anthony Browne. Reprinted by permission of Doubleday, a
division of Bantam Doubleday Dell Publishing Group, Inc.

Acknowledgments appear on page 148.

Printed in the U.S.A.

ISBN: 0-395-61081-8

3456789-D-96 95 94 93

Bears Don't Go To School

Senior Author
John J. Pikulski

Senior Coordinating Author
J. David Cooper

Senior Consulting Author
William K. Durr

Coordinating Authors
Kathryn H. Au
M. Jean Greenlaw
Marjorie Y. Lipson
Susan E. Page
Sheila W. Valencia
Karen K. Wixson

Authors
Rosalinda B. Barrera
Edwina Bradley
Ruth P. Bunyan
Jacqueline L. Chaparro
Jacqueline C. Comas
Alan N. Crawford
Robert L. Hillerich
Timothy G. Johnson
Jana M. Mason
Pamela A. Mason
William E. Nagy
Joseph S. Renzulli
Alfredo Schifini

Senior Advisor
Richard C. Anderson

Advisors
Christopher J. Baker
Charles Peters
Mary Ellen Vogt

HOUGHTON MIFFLIN COMPANY   BOSTON
Atlanta   Dallas   Geneva, Illinois   Palo Alto   Princeton   Toronto

Award Winner

Do you think working together is fun, or hard to do? Sometimes it's a little of both.

Here are some stories and poems about people who work together — and about some funny things that happen to them.

WORKING TOGETHER

Big Book

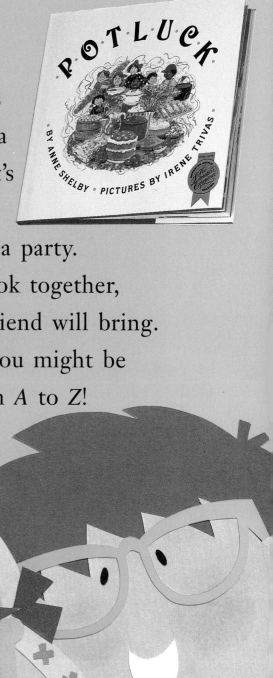

Imagine all your friends working together to make a giant potluck dinner. That's what happens when the children in this story have a party.

When you read this book together, you can guess what each friend will bring. By the time you're done, you might be hungry for everything from *A* to *Z*!

A story from

Punky Spends the Day

by Sally G. Ward

Raking Leaves

Punky put on her coat and ran outside.
"Grampy, wait for me!"

They raked and raked.

Punky worked hard
at being helpful.

15

Sometimes
the leaves went
into the basket . . .

and sometimes
they didn't.

Sometimes
the leaves went
onto the tarp . . .

and sometimes
they didn't.

17

They raked for a long time.
"Grampy, I want to stop now."

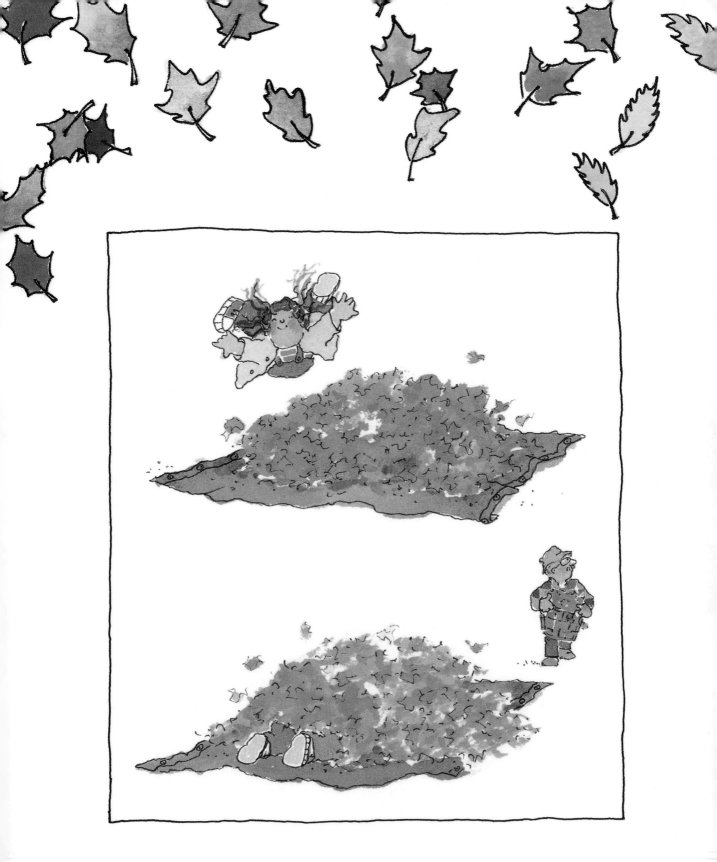

"Goodness, these leaves are heavy!"

surprise!

FUN ways to help OUT

Punky had fun while she was helping her grandfather rake leaves. Can you think of some ways to make working together more fun?

Make a list of some ways you help out at home or at school. Draw some pictures to show how to make these jobs more fun. Try out your new ideas the next time you're helping out!

Meet the Author and Illustrator

Sally Ward remembers how much she liked
to hide when she was little, just like Punky!
Mrs. Ward is a grandmother now. She has
written and drawn the pictures for two
other storybooks, *Molly and Grandma* and
Charlie and Grandma.

The Mulberry Bush

a traditional singing game
illustrated by Ashley Wolff

Here we go round the mulberry bush, The mulberry bush, the mulberry bush. Here we go round the mulberry bush, So early in the morning.

This is the way
　　we dig and rake,
Dig and rake,
　　dig and rake.
This is the way
　　we dig and rake,
So early Monday
　　morning.

This is the way
　　we plant the seeds,
Plant the seeds,
　　plant the seeds.
This is the way
　　we plant the seeds,
So early Tuesday
　　morning.

This is the way
    we water the garden,
Water the garden,
    water the garden.
This is the way
    we water the garden,
So early Wednesday
    morning.

This is the way
    we pound the stakes,
Pound the stakes,
    pound the stakes.
This is the way
    we pound the stakes,
So early Thursday
    morning.

This is the way
  we shoo the birds,
Shoo the birds,
  shoo the birds.
This is the way
  we shoo the birds,
So early Friday
  morning.

This is the way
  we weed and hoe,
Weed and hoe,
  weed and hoe.
This is the way
  we weed and hoe,
So early Saturday
  morning.

This is the way
  we shout "Hurray!"
Shout "Hurray!"
  Shout "Hurray!"
This is the way
  we shout "Hurray!"
So early Sunday
  morning.

Here we go round the mulberry bush, So early in the morning.

Sophie and Jack Help Out

by Judy Taylor   illustrated by Susan Gantner

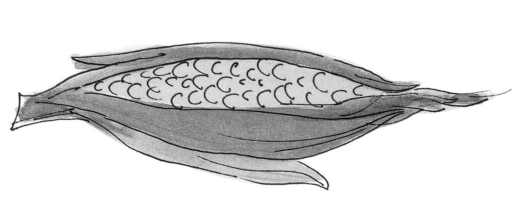

30

Spring had arrived.

But everyone was worried.

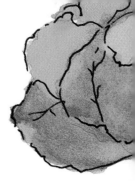

Papa could not plant the vegetables.

He was not well.

"I'll do it," said Sophie.

"I'll help," said Jack.

So they dug

and they weeded,

39

they raked

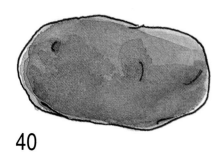

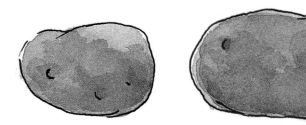

and they planted.

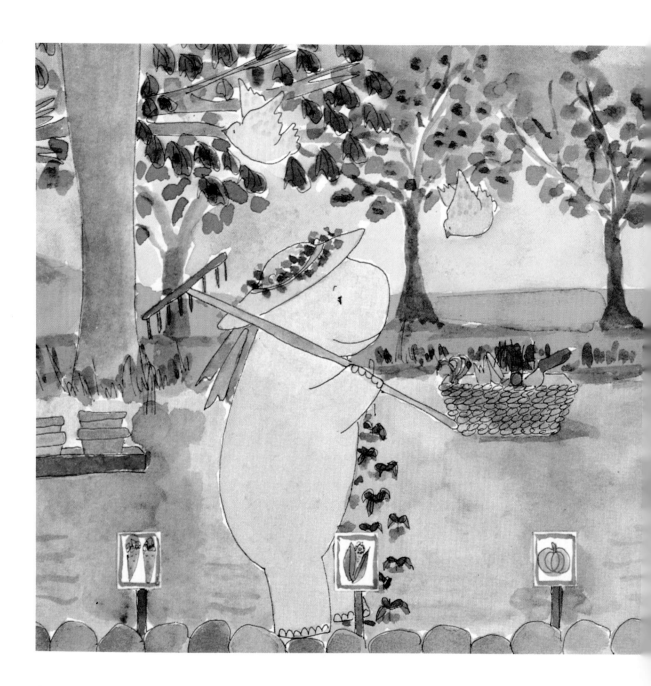

Soon it was all done.

But that night the wind roared

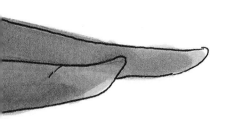

and the rain poured.

The garden was a mess.

"I'll fix it," said Jack.

"I'll help," said Sophie.

49

When the vegetables were ready

there were many surprises.

Can you see why?

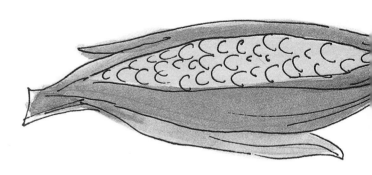

Help Out With Signs

To help find each vegetable, Sophie and Jack put up signs in the garden. Work together to make signs for the classroom. Put your signs up where they can help someone!

Meet the Author

Sophie and Jack Help Out is the second storybook by Judy Taylor. She also wrote a third one, *Sophie and Jack in the Snow*.

Mrs. Taylor is a grandmother now, but she still likes to read storybooks. One of her favorites is *Peter Rabbit* by Beatrix Potter. She likes it so much that she has written three books about the author!

Meet the Illustrator

Susan Gantner studied painting in art school. Today she is best known for her paintings of animals on greeting cards. Sophie and Jack have appeared on some of her cards, but Ms. Gantner also likes to paint pictures of cats and bears.

Some of her cards are shown here.

My Dad And I

My Dad and I
made shavings fly:
we built a shelf for books,
and planed a door
and patched the floor
and put up several hooks,
and plugged a leak
and oiled a squeak
and got a toaster wired.
I hoped we might
keep on all night . . .
but Dad got AWFULLY tired.

by Aileen Fisher

Wonderful
Dinner

I set the table
I made it all neat,
And everyone said
When they sat down to eat,
"The table looks pretty.
You did it just right."

It was a wonderful
Dinner that night!

by Leland B. Jacobs

Bones, Bones,

by Byron Barton

Dinosaur Bones

Bones. Bones. We look for bones.

Tyrannosaurus, Apatosaurus,
Stegosaurus, Ankylosaurus,
Parasaurolophus, Gallimimus,
Thecodontosaurus, Triceratops.

We look for the bones of dinosaurs.

We find them.

We dig them up.

We wrap them

and pack them.

We load them on trucks.

We have the bones of dinosaurs.

We have head bones, foot bones,
leg bones, rib bones, back bones,
teeth and claws.

We put the claws on the foot bones

and the foot bones on the leg bones.

We put the teeth in the head bones

and the head bones
on the neck bones.

We put the rib bones

on the back bones.

And the tail bones are last.

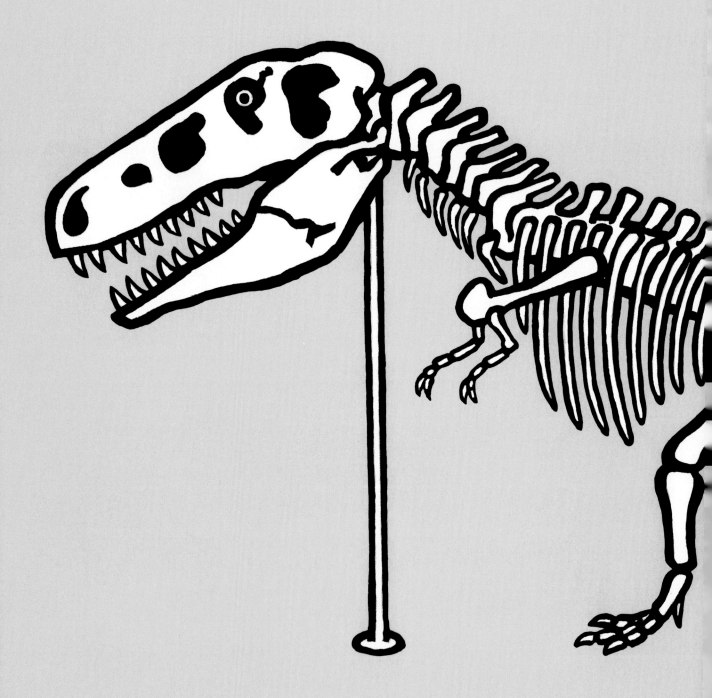

These are the bones
of Tyrannosaurus rex.

Bones. Bones. We look for bones.

We look for the bones of dinosaurs.

Make a Dinosaur Poster

What dinosaur would you like to learn more about?

Find some information on this dinosaur. Then get together with some friends and make a dinosaur poster. Write a sentence about something you learned, and share it with the class.

■ Meet the ━━━━ Author and Illustrator

Byron Barton always wanted to be an artist. When he was a little boy, he liked to paint pictures of Native Americans.

When Mr. Barton grew up, he went to art school in California. Since then, he has written and drawn the pictures for many books, including *Where's Al?* and *Buzz Buzz Buzz*. He lives in New York City.

Company

I'm fixing a lunch for a dinosaur.
Who knows when one might come by?
I'm pulling up all the weeds I can find.
I'm piling them high as the sky.
I'm fixing a lunch for a dinosaur.
I hope he will stop by soon.
Maybe he'll just walk down my street
And have some lunch at noon.

by Bobbi Katz

Good Books That Work Together

Potluck *by Anne Shelby*

Together you read about the alphabetical feast in this book. Now read it again, and see if you can recall which dish goes with each letter of the alphabet.

Helping Out *by George Ancona*

These girls and boys help out with everything from cooking to changing the oil in a car. Imagine yourself as a helper, too!

Busy Monday Morning *by Janina Domanska*

A boy works with his father on something different every day of the week. Sing this song along with them and find out what they do.

Peanut Butter and Jelly

by Nadine Bernard Westcott

Find out how the children in this book make a HUGE peanut butter and jelly sandwich — with a little help from their friends.

Ten Little Rabbits

by Virginia Grossman and Sylvia Long

Ten rabbits work together on Native American arts such as weaving and storytelling. You'll enjoy following the rhymes in this book.

SOMETHING SPECIAL

Do you have something that is special to you? It could be a special friend, a special toy, a special pet — a special anything!

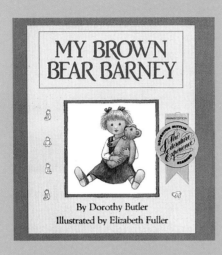

Big Book

This book is about a girl who takes her special bear everywhere she goes!

Read this book together. Find out what the girl does with her bear when school begins.

Contents

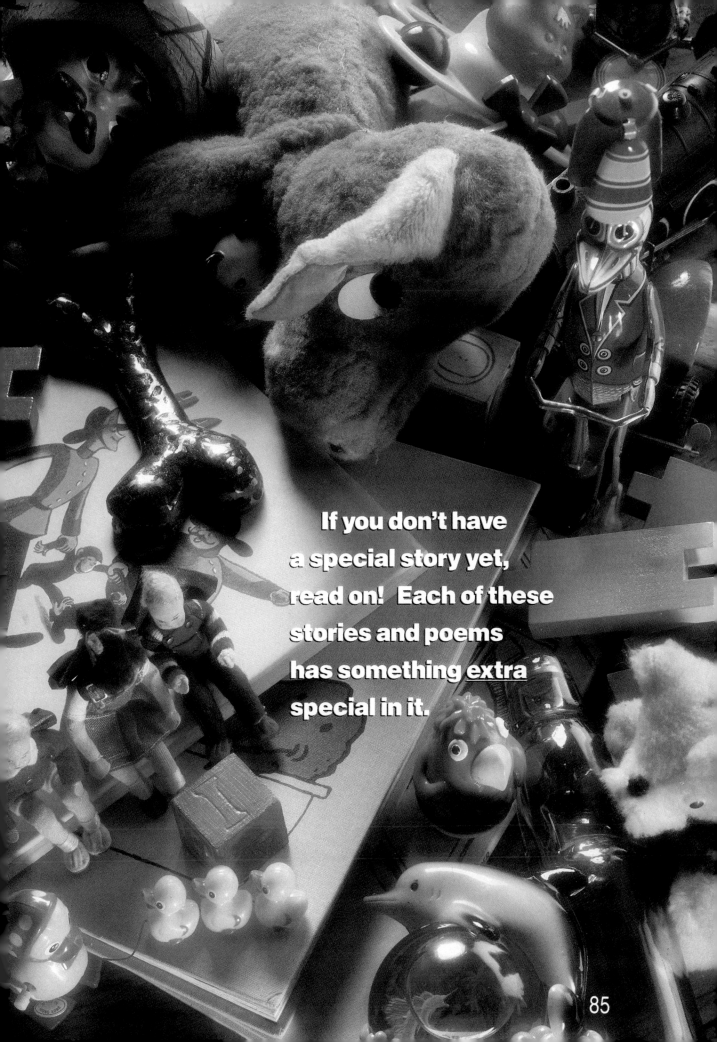

If you don't have
a special story yet,
read on! Each of these
stories and poems
has something extra
special in it.

If I had a pig
MICK INKPEN

If I had a pig…

I would tell him…

…a joke.

I would hide from him...
...and jump out.

Boo!

We could make a house…
…and have our friends sleep over.

We could paint pictures…
…of each other.

We could have fights...

...and piggybacks.

On his birthday...
...I would bake him a cake.

I would race him...
...to the park.

93

If it snowed...
...I would make him a snowpig.

We would need our boots…
…if it rained.

We could stay in the bath...
...until we wrinkled up.

I would read him a story...
...and take him to bed.

A SPECIAL FRIEND

Did the boy in this story really
have a pig, or did he just imagine one?
Would you like to have a pig or
some other special animal friend?
Write about something that you and
your friend could do together. Draw
a picture, too.

Meet the Author and Illustrator

Mick Inkpen has written and drawn the pictures for another storybook about a special animal friend, *If I Had a Sheep*. He and his partner, Nick Butterworth, have worked on over twenty books together. They also helped produce a children's television program in England called "Rub-a-Dub-Tub."

If I Had A Dinosaur

a song by Raffi

words by Raffi, D. Pike, and B. & B. Simpson

illustrated by Don Stuart

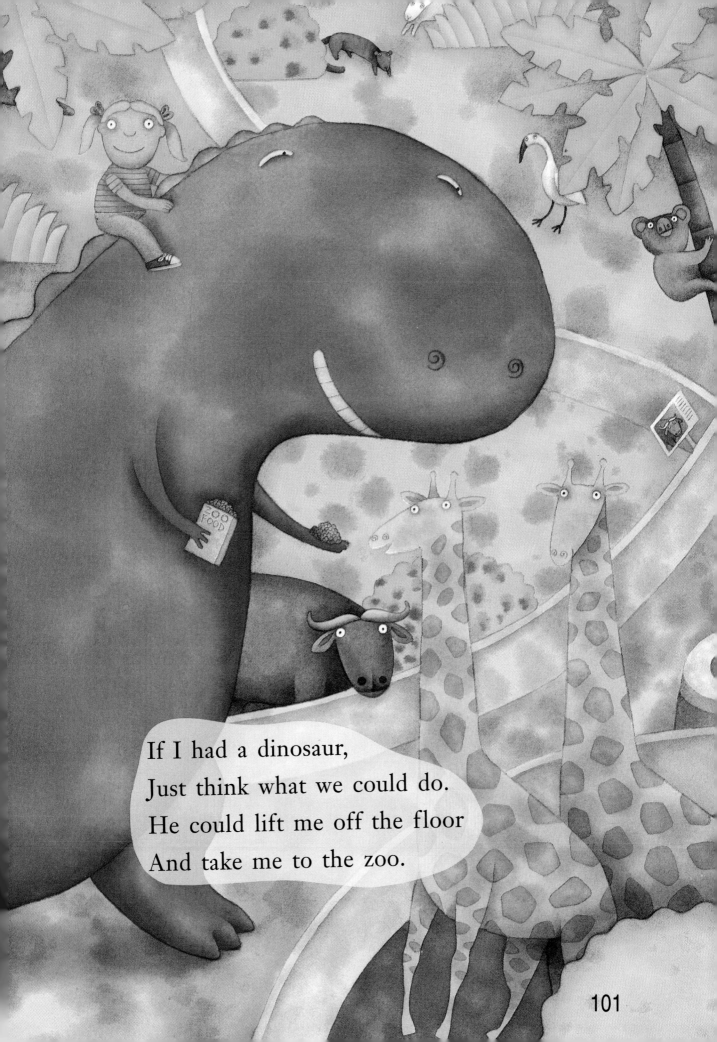

If I had a dinosaur,
Just think what we could do.
He could lift me off the floor
And take me to the zoo.

If I had a dinosaur,
Just think what we could see.
We could look inside the cloud
Above my balcony.

102

And if I had a dinosaur,
Just think where we could go.
All the way to Grandma's house
To play her piano.

104

105

If I Had A Dinosaur

If I had a di-no-saur, just think what we could

do.   He could lift me off the floor and

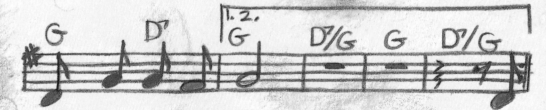

take me to the zoo.

Good Books, Good Times!

Good books.
Good times.
Good stories.
Good rhymes.
Good beginnings.
Good ends.
Good people.
Good friends.
Good fiction.
Good facts.
Good adventures.
Good acts.
Good stories.
Good rhymes.
Good books.
Good times.

by Lee Bennett Hopkins

Jeannette Caines

I NEED A LUNCH BOX

pictures by
Pat Cummings

My sister Doris got a brand new
lunch box.
I need a lunch box too.
But Mommy said no lunch box until
I start school.

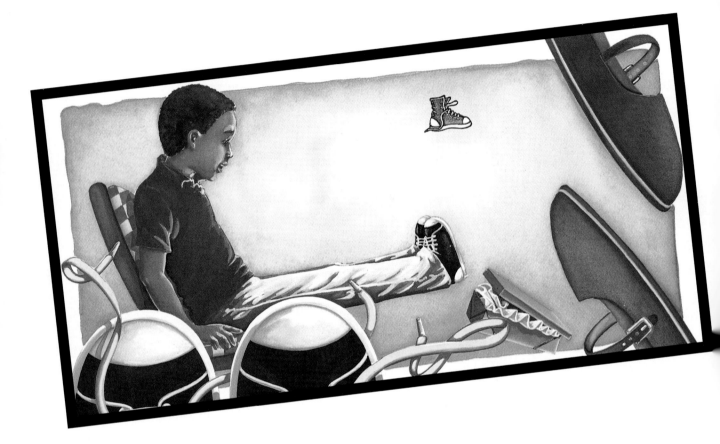

Last week Daddy bought us new shoes.
Brown school shoes for Doris.
Black sneakers with yellow laces for me.

We walked past the lunch box counter,
twice.
I need a lunch box!

Doris got a pencil case with a ruler,
two new pencils, and two pink erasers.

All I got was a coloring book about
space men and a box of crayons —
but no lunch box.

Yesterday Doris got book covers, a
raincoat, and an umbrella — all because
she's going to first grade.

If I had a lunch box I could keep
my crayons in it. Or my marbles,
or bug collection, or toy animals.

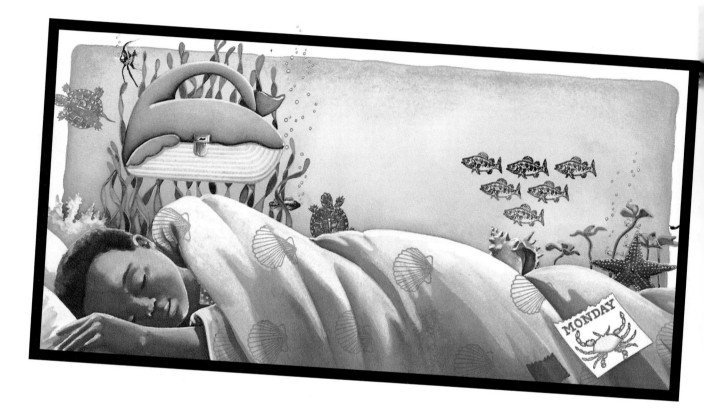

I dreamed I had five lunch boxes,
one for every day.
Blue for Monday . . .

Green for Tuesday . . .

Red for Wednesday . . .

Purple for Thursday . . .

Yellow for Friday.

I filled them with peanut butter and jelly
sandwiches, apples, oranges, chocolate
cake, cookies and pies and donuts.
And then we had a lunch box parade.

Doris starts school today.
I felt sorta bad when Mommy handed
Doris her brand new lunch box.
But then Daddy said, "I have a surprise
for you."

Wow!

I got a lunch box too!

Make a Calendar

The boy in this story dreamed about having a different lunch box for every day of the week.

Make a one-week calendar. Under each day, write a sentence about something special you would like to do and draw a picture. Then hang your calendar where you can see it every day.

Meet the Author

Jeannette Caines was born in New York City. *I Need a Lunch Box* is her fifth book for children. Two of her other books are *Window Wishing* and *Just Us Women*.

Ms. Caines is married and has two children. Many of her stories are about family life.

Meet the Illustrator

Pat Cummings was born in Chicago. When she was little, she liked to draw pictures of ballerinas. After she went to art school, Ms. Cummings worked as an artist for a children's theater.

Pat Cummings also writes books, as well as drawing the pictures for them. Two of the books she has written are *C.L.O.U.D.S.* and *Jimmy Lee Did It*.

A Friendship Bridge

by Graciela Peña

I want to build a bridge,
A bridge from friend to friend.
I want to build a bridge,
A bridge that will not end.

From Mama's hand to Papa's,
To Vince and Ana too,
My bridge would grow and grow
From friendships old and new.

I want to build a bridge,
A bridge from friend to friend.
I want to build a bridge,
A bridge that will not end.

translated from Spanish

My Teddy Bear

A teddy bear is a faithful friend.
You can pick him up at either end.
His fur is the color
    of breakfast toast,
And he's always there
    when you need him most.

by Marchette Chute

Daniel Goes Fishing

by Robert and Estella Menchaca

illustrated by Pamela Rossi

Roberto and Daniel woke up early.
They were going fishing with Papa!
It was Daniel's first time to go along.

Roberto and Papa got ready . . .

And Daniel just watched.

Roberto and Papa made
a big breakfast . . .

And Daniel just watched.

Roberto and Papa got
the fishing box . . .

And Daniel just watched.

Roberto and Papa began to fish
at the river . . .

134

And Daniel just watched.

Roberto and Papa didn't catch any fish —
but the fish ate the bait!

And Daniel just watched.

Roberto and Papa took a nap . . .

And Daniel just watched.

Then Daniel walked over
and grabbed the rod. He began
to fish, and right away . . .

he caught the **biggest** fish
anyone had ever seen . . .

and everyone just watched HIM!

That's Special!

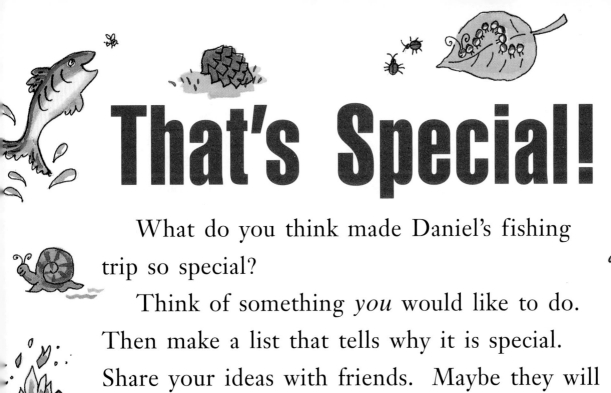

What do you think made Daniel's fishing trip so special?

Think of something *you* would like to do. Then make a list that tells why it is special. Share your ideas with friends. Maybe they will think that's special, too!

Meet the Authors

Robert Menchaca, a kindergarten teacher, and his wife, Estella, work as a writing team. *Daniel Goes Fishing* was written after a family fishing trip. The Menchacas live in Seguin, Texas, with their sons Daniel and Roberto.

Meet the Illustrator

Pamela Rossi has loved drawing pictures since she was a little girl. She enjoys many other things, too. She loves to travel and swim in the ocean. She even parachutes out of airplanes! Pamela Rossi lives in Evanston, Illinois.

ARE THESE SPECIAL?

OODLES OF NOODLES

I love noodles. Give me oodles.

Make a mound up to the sun.

Noodles are my favorite foodles.

I eat noodles by the ton.

by Lucia and James L. Hymes, Jr.

BUGS

I am very fond of bugs.

I kiss them

And I give them hugs.

by Karla Kuskin

Special! Special!

My Brown Bear Barney

by Dorothy Butler

The girl in this story takes her bear everywhere — even to the beach! As you read this story again, see if you can remember what else she takes with her.

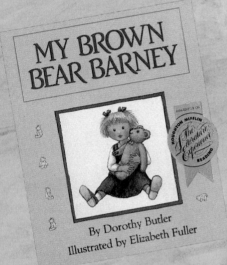

Bread Bread Bread

by Ann Morris

Do you know how many different kinds of bread people eat? This book will show you with photographs from all over the world.

Read All About It!

Monster Can't Sleep
by *Virginia Mueller*

It's bedtime, but Monster isn't sleepy. What will happen when Monster finds his special toy spider?

Secret Valentine
by *Catherine Stock*

After the girl in this book sends some valentines, she gets a secret valentine in return. Who could have sent it?

Read Alone Books

Ian's Pet
My New Glasses
The Bike Race

Acknowledgments

For each of the selections listed below, grateful acknowledgment is made for permission to excerpt and/or reprint original or copyrighted material, as follows:

Major Selections

Bones, Bones, Dinosaur Bones by Byron Barton. Copyright © 1990 by Byron Barton. Reprinted by permission of HarperCollins Publishers.

I Need a Lunch Box by Jeannette Caines, illustrated by Pat Cummings. Text copyright © 1988 by Jeannette Franklin Caines. Illustrations copyright © 1988 by Pat Cummings. Reprinted by permission of HarperCollins Publishers.

"If I Had a Dinosaur," words and music by Raffi, D. Pike, B. & B. Simpson. Copyright © 1978 by Homeland Publishing, a division of Troubadour Records, Ltd. From *The Raffi Singable Songbook* (Crown/Random House Publishers). Reprinted by permission.

If I Had a Pig by Mick Inkpen. Copyright © 1988 by Mick Inkpen. Reprinted by Macmillan Children's Books, a division of Macmillan Publishers, Ltd.

"Raking Leaves" from *Punky Spends the Day* by Sally G. Ward. Copyright © 1989 by Sally G. Ward. Reprinted by permission of the publisher, Dutton Children's Books, a division of Penguin Books USA, Inc.

Sophie and Jack Help Out, text copyright © 1983 by Judy Taylor, illustrations copyright © 1983 by Susan Gantner. Reprinted by permission of Philomel Books, and The Bodley Head.

Poetry

"Bugs" from *Dogs and Dragons, Trees and Dreams* by Karla Kuskin. Originally published in *Alexander Soames: His Poems* by Karla Kuskin. Copyright © 1962 by Karla Kuskin. Reprinted by permission of Harper and Row, Publishers, Inc.

"Company" from *Upside Down and Inside Out: Poems For All Your Pockets* by Bobbi Katz. Copyright © 1973 by Bobbi Katz. Reprinted by permission of the author.

"A Friendship Bridge" by Graciela Peña. Reprinted by permission of the author.

"Good Books, Good Times!" from *More Surprises* by Lee Bennett Hopkins. Copyright © 1985 by Lee Bennett Hopkins. Reprinted by permission of Curtis Brown, Ltd.

"My Dad and I" from *Runny Days, Sunny Days* by Aileen Fisher. Copyright © 1958 by Aileen Fisher; copyright renewed. Reprinted by permission of the author, who controls rights.

"My Teddy Bear" from *Rhymes About Us* by Marchette Chute. Copyright © 1974 by E. P. Dutton, Inc. Reprinted by permission of Mary Chute Smith.

"Oodles of Noodles" from *Oodles of Noodles* by Lucia and James L. Hymes, Jr. Copyright © 1964, Addison Wesley Publishing Co., Inc., Reading, Massachusetts. Reprinted with permission of the publisher.

"Wonderful Dinner" from *All About Me: Verses I Can Read* by Leland B. Jacobs. Copyright © 1971 by Leland B. Jacobs. Reprinted by permission of Leland B. Jacobs.

Credits

Program Design Carbone Smolan Associates

Cover Design Carbone Smolan Associates

Design 8–11, 23, 58–81 John Morning Design, Inc.; 12–22, 24, 25, 30–55 Joshua Hayes; 82–147 Studio Izbickas

Introduction (left to right) 1st row: Joshua Hayes; Don Stuart; Don Stuart; 2nd row: Ashley Wolff; Roy Marsh/The Stock Market; Ashley Wolff; 3rd row: Don Stuart; Ashley Wolff; John Lei; 4th row: Shari Halpern; John Lei; Victoria Chess

Table of Contents 4 Pau Estrada; 6 Courtesy FAO Schwarz

Illustration 8–11 Mary Thelen; 12–22 Sally G. Ward (*Punky*); Marie Anne McCue (leaves); 24–29 Ashley Wolff; 30–53 Susan Gantner (*Sophie and Jack*); Charles Ragins (vegetables); 54 Sal Murdocca; 56–57 Joshua Hayes; 58–76 Byron Barton; 77 Mary Thelen; 79 Pau Estrada; 80–81 Mary Thelen; 86–97 Mick Inkpen; 98 Richard Martin; 99 Mick Inkpen; 100–105 Don Stuart; 106 D. C. Langer; 108–123, 125 Pat Cummings; 124 Shari Halpern; 126–127 Susan Guevara; 129–142 Pamela Rossi; 143 Ellen Joy Sesaki; 144 Studio Izbickas; 145 Victoria Chess; 146–147 Shari Halpern

Photography 23 Photo by Jacqueline Bauer, Courtesy of Sally Ward (top left); 78 Reprinted courtesy of HarperCollins Children's Books; 82 R. Llewellyn/Superstock; 82 John Running/TSW-CLICK/Chicago Ltd. (bottom); 83 Marleen Ferguson/TSW-CLICK/Chicago Ltd. (top right); 83 T. Rosenthal/Superstock (top left); 83 Bob Daemmrich (bottom); 85 Jim Sherer; 107 Jim Sherer; 107 Bob Daemmrich/TSW-CLICK/Chicago Ltd. (bottom left); 125 Reprinted courtesy of HarperCollins Children's Books, Photo: Percidia (bottom); 125 Reprinted courtesy of HarperCollins Children's Books, Photo: Al Cetta (top); 128 Courtesy of FAO Schwarz; 144 Courtesy Robert and Estella Menchaca (top); 144 Courtesy of Pamela Rossi (bottom); 145 Roy Morsch/The Stock Market